HOOK'S CREW

PETER PAN

TINKER BELL

For information regarding permission, write to:
Disney Licensed Publishing,
114 Fifth Avenue, New York, New York 10011

0-7172-6980-9

Printed in the U.S.A.
First printing, July 2004

DISNEP

TINKER BELL'S
SECRET ADVENTURE

SCHOLASTIC INC.

New York   Toronto   London   Auckland   Sydney
Mexico City   New Delhi   Hong Kong   Buenos Aires

The pixie Tinker Bell loved living in Never Land with Peter Pan and the Lost Boys. They spent their days doing whatever they wanted—most of the time that meant playing some kind of game.

Usually this was wonderful for all of them. But lately, Tinker Bell had been less interested in games.

Finally one afternoon, Tinker Bell stopped playing and jingled quietly to herself, wishing she could tell Peter how she felt. But how would she ever make Peter understand that what she really wanted was her own adventure?

What Tinker Bell didn't realize was that she was about to get her wish. . . .

At that same moment, aboard his pirate ship, the *Jolly Roger*, Captain Hook was very angry with his first mate, Smee. "Why didn't you catch Peter Pan when you had the chance?" Hook roared at Smee.

"But . . . but . . . ," Smee stammered. He wanted to say that he'd been too busy trying to save Captain Hook, after he had been thrown overboard by Peter and almost eaten by the dreaded, hungry Crocodile. But Smee knew better than to remind the Captain.

So Smee decided the only way to make the Captain happy was to catch Peter Pan. "But how?" Smee wondered. He thought and he thought.

Eventually, Smee had an idea. "I'll snatch Peter's little pixie friend, Tinker Bell," Smee decided. "If I catch her, we'll be able to trap Peter Pan when he comes to save Tinker Bell."

Determined, Smee set off to find and capture the unsuspecting pixie.

Deep in the forest, Smee found a glittering trail. "Aha!" he exclaimed. "This must be Tinker Bell's pixie dust."

Excited, Smee followed the trail—right to the flower where Tinker Bell lay daydreaming.

Smee quietly crept closer. Just as he was about to catch her in a tiny box—

"Ah-choo!" Smee sneezed.

Startled but too sleepy to notice Smee, Tinker Bell flew quickly away to a soft lily pad near the water's edge.

A little later, Smee found her again.

"Good—this time she looks asleep," he thought. "I'll snag the lily pad with this stick and pull her to shore." So he stretched and he stretched. "Just . . . a little . . . more—"

SPLASH!

When Smee surfaced, Tinker Bell had disappeared.

Now soaking wet and discouraged, Smee gave up and set off for the *Jolly Roger.* "I'll just have to think of another way to please Captain Hook."

Just then Smee spotted the tiny pixie smelling a flower. Thinking quickly, he swooped down and scooped up Tinker Bell in his net!

"I did it, I did it!" cheered a triumphant Smee. Finally, Captain Hook would know that Smee was a loyal pirate.

But when Smee looked at Tinker Bell, he noticed
that her eyes were closed and she wasn't moving!
Even worse, the pixie's light had started to fade.
Smee panicked!

"Oh no, she must have fainted!" Smee cried.
"Miss Bell, wake up."

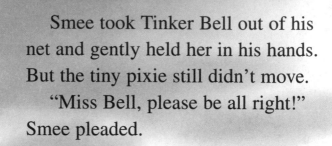

Smee took Tinker Bell out of his
net and gently held her in his hands.
But the tiny pixie still didn't move.
"Miss Bell, please be all right!"
Smee pleaded.

A second later Tinker Bell stirred a little bit.
Just as her light started to glow brighter, her eyes
fluttered open.

Tinker Bell felt better.
She stretched her wings,
flew into the air, and
then landed back in
Smee's hand.

Smee was so relieved. "Whew! I'm
so glad you're okay," he said, smiling.

But suddenly Tinker Bell recognized Smee. Before she could escape, Smee tightened his grip and wouldn't let her go.

"Oh no. You're coming with me!" he declared.

Tinker Bell was terrified that she might never see her friends again. She had to get free! Perhaps she could distract Smee somehow. . . .

As the pirate
passed by a bush,
Tinker Bell leaned
over, picked a pretty
flower, and gave it
to Smee.

Smee had never been given a flower before. He
sniffed it and smiled. "Mmm, I didn't know that flowers
smelled so sweet!" he admitted to Tinker Bell.

Tinker Bell climbed onto Smee's shoulder, jingled innocently, and pointed to a flock of birds high in the sky.

Looking up, Smee said, "What beautiful birds! Why, I can see a blue one, a green one, and even some purple ones!" Smee exclaimed.

Tinker Bell smiled. Smee was thinking happy thoughts. And that gave her another idea.

Tinker Bell sprinkled
some pixie dust over Smee.
Suddenly the pirate
floated into the air.
Amazed, Smee
shouted, "Look at
me, Miss Bell. I can fly!"
Tinker Bell giggled. Smee was the
biggest, fattest bird she had ever seen!

"Oh, if Captain Hook could see me now," cried Smee.

But the thought of Captain Hook was *not* a happy thought.

All of a sudden Smee stopped flying and began to fall to the ground. "H-E-L-P!" he cried.

And to Tinker Bell's dismay, he landed right on . . .

. . . Captain Hook! *Splat!*

"Ugh. Get off me, you nincompoop!" the Captain roared. "What are you doing?"

"I'm so sorry, Cap'n! I was . . . uh . . . ," Smee stammered, as he struggled to sit up.

"Well, well," Captain Hook said gleefully when he spotted Tinker Bell. "Who have we here?"

Captain Hook swooped her up in his hat. "Gotcha!" he cried meanly.

Tinker Bell bravely struggled to fight her way out of the hat. But no matter how hard she tried, she couldn't get free.

"Poor Tinker Bell," Smee thought to himself.

"Well done, Smee!" Captain Hook sneered. "We'll use Miss Bell as bait! Peter Pan's as good as mine!"

Smee unhappily followed as Captain Hook hurried back to the *Jolly Roger*, clutching Tinker Bell in his hat.

"Three cheers for the Captain!" shouted the other pirates when Hook showed them the pixie.

"He won't use me to lure Peter and the Lost Boys to this ship," Tinker Bell vowed.

But Captain Hook pushed her into a birdcage and slammed the door. "It's the perfect pixie prison!" he exclaimed. "Luckily for you, the parrot is no longer in it!" he snarled at the pixie.

Then Captain Hook laughed and slipped the key into his pocket.

He bowed to Tinker Bell. "Excuse me, my dear Miss Bell. I'm going below deck to write a letter to your precious Peter Pan!"

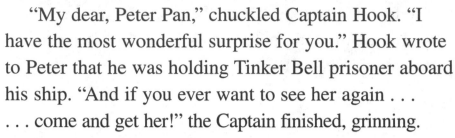

"My dear, Peter Pan," chuckled Captain Hook. "I have the most wonderful surprise for you." Hook wrote to Peter that he was holding Tinker Bell prisoner aboard his ship. "And if you ever want to see her again . . . . . . come and get her!" the Captain finished, grinning.

Certain that Peter would come, Hook was determined to be ready. The Captain hadn't enjoyed himself so much in ages!

Later, a carrier pigeon delivered Captain Hook's letter to the underground tree house where Peter Pan and the Lost Boys lived.

Peter read it aloud to the others. "Hook can't do this!" Peter shouted.

"But he already has . . . ," Nibs sadly pointed out.

"We'll see about that. Follow me, men!" Peter cried.

Peter and the Lost Boys flew as quickly as they could towards the *Jolly Roger*. Peter was going to free Tinker Bell. He wasn't going to let his little friend down—she needed him!

"We're not leaving without Tink," Peter vowed.

Meanwhile, Smee was
apologizing to Tinker
Bell. "I didn't want
things to turn out this
way," Smee tried to
explain. "Well, I did. . . .
But then I didn't!"

Suddenly a dark shadow loomed over Tinker Bell's cage. "Careful, Smee," a big, mean pirate warned when he overheard Smee. "Just think what Captain Hook will do to you if you unlock the cage."

Smee knew Captain Hook would make his life miserable. So Smee did what he had to do. "I'd never unlock the cage," Smee callcd to the other pirate as he left. Then Smee left, too.

Tiny Tinker Bell was crushed. She had hoped Smee was different from the other pirates. But it seemed she was wrong.

Suddenly Tinker Bell heard a noise. The cage started to shake. Tinker Bell grabbed the bars. What was happening?

Then Tinker Bell looked down and noticed a tiny hole being cut into the floor of the cage! Tinker Bell knelt down and saw Smee staring at her with a tiny file in his hand.

"I guess no one noticed this hole that the parrot must have pecked in the bottom of the cage," pretended Smee.

The hole was just big enough for Tinker Bell to squeeze through. Very thankful and excited, she spread her wings and started to fly away.

"Ahoy, the pixie's out of the cage!" shouted a pirate.

Quickly the pirates surrounded her.

Just then Peter and the Lost Boys soared into sight.
"If you hurt Tink, you'll answer to me!" shouted Peter.
Captain Hook rushed up. "Why, it's Peter Pan, my
old friend. I knew you would come!" gushed Hook.

Captain Hook then grinned and
waved his sharp sword. "But you
won't be leaving!"

Captain Hook shouted to his men, "Come on, you lazy sea dogs. This time, let's get them!"

Peter and the Lost Boys bravely faced the pirates. Peter laughed. "You never learn, Hook!"

Able to slip away, Tinker Bell raced to the top of the main sail and loosened it. Instantly the huge sail started to fall.

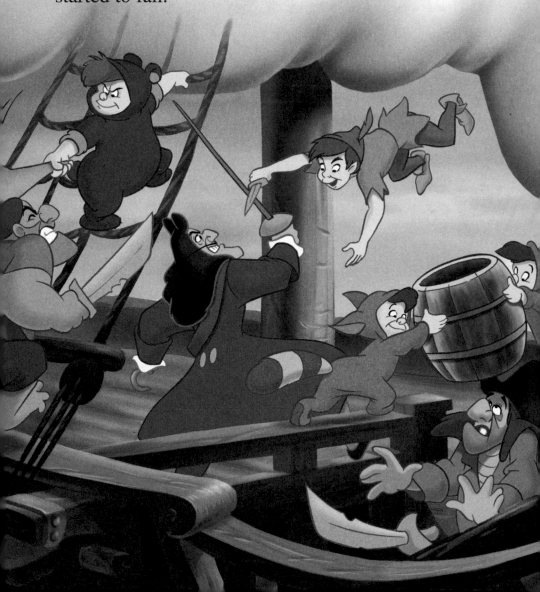

Peter saw the sail tumbling
and shouted to the Lost Boys,
"Save yourselves!"

The Lost Boys leapt out of
the way just in time!

The pirates weren't so lucky. The heavy sail
fell on top of them and trapped them underneath.
Peter and the Lost Boys jumped for joy. They
cheered, "Hooray for Tinker Bell!"

"Not so fast, Pan!"
snarled Captain Hook,
as he crawled out. "I
haven't finished with
you yet!"

Hook lunged at Peter, and the two started fighting. Captain Hook's long sword inched closer and closer to Peter.

When Captain Hook jumped onto a pile of rope, Tinker Bell grabbed the end of the rope.

As she tugged hard, the rope came undone. Captain Hook lost his balance. He teetered towards the side of the ship and . . .

Splash! Captain Hook hit the water.

When Captain Hook bobbed to the surface, he heard the dreaded sound. . . .

Tick tock—tick tock—TICK TOCK!

Suddenly Captain Hook was staring at the Crocodile's pointy teeth. "Oh no, not you again!" the Captain wailed.

The hungry Crocodile snapped at Captain Hook as he paddled frantically away.

"You don't want to hurt me," Hook pleaded, desperately trying to get away.

"Better hurry, Hook!" Peter shouted. "The Croc is getting closer!"

"Is there anything I can do, Cap'n?" Smee called over the side of the ship.

"You can rescue me and capture Pan!" Captain Hook shouted back.

"But I can only do one thing at a time!" Smee yelled.

"Then save me, you fool!" Hook screeched.

Turning to the Lost Boys and Tinker Bell, Peter said, "Come on, it's time to go home."

Smee threw a rope to Captain Hook and tugged him up out of the water— just as the Crocodile clamped its jaws around one of the Captain's shoes.

"I'll get you, Peter Pan!" vowed Hook, shaking his fist.

"You said that the last time," Peter yelled, laughing. "And look where that got you!"

Tinker Bell flew past Smee, who winked at her. Tinker Bell would always be grateful to her new friend for saving her.

Meanwhile, Smee knew that Captain Hook must never find out how the pixie really escaped.

It would be Smee's and Tinker Bell's best-kept secret.

Peter and the Lost Boys
were thrilled to have Tinker
Bell back safely.

"How did Hook catch you
in the first place, Tink?"
Peter asked.

Smiling, Tinker Bell
jingled and jingled. In fact,
she jingled so quickly that
Peter couldn't understand
what she was saying.

Tinker Bell had finally had her own adventure.
Jingling loudly and happily, she flew ahead of the rest.

"Come on, boys!" Peter shouted. "Tink says, 'Let's
go home!'"